Jeremy in the **Underworld**

Becky Citra

with illustrations by Jessica Milne

ORCA BOOK PUBLISHERS

To the boys and girls at Bridge Lake School. —B.C.
To my husband Greg, and our newborn son Thomas. —J.M.

Text copyright © 2006 Becky Citra
Interior illustrations copyright © 2006 Jessica Milne

Library and Archives Canada Cataloguing in Publication

Citra, Becky
Jeremy in the underworld / Becky Citra; with illustrations by Jessica Milne.

(Orca echoes)
Sequel to: Jeremy and the enchanted theater.
ISBN 1-55143-466-0

I. Milne, Jessica, 1974- II. Title. III. Series.

PS8555.I87J474 2006   jC813'.54   C2006-900340-8

First Published inthe United States: 2006
Library of Congress Control Number:2006920832

Summary: In this sequel to *Jeremy and the Enchanted Theater*,
Jeremy and Aristotle must journey into the world of the dead.

Orca Book Publishers gratefully acknowledges the support for its publishing programs
provided by the following agencies: the Government of Canada through the Department
of Canadian Heritage'sBook Publishing Industry Development Program (BPIDP),
the Canada Council for the Arts, and the British Columbia Arts Council.

Design by Lynn O'Rourke

Orca Book Publishers
P.O. Box 5626, Stn.B
Victoria, BC Canada
V8R 6S4

Orca Book Publishers
PO Box 468
Custer, WA USA
98240-0468

Printed and bound in Canada

09 08 07 06 • 5 4 3 2 1

Chapter One
The Riddle

"I'm back!" said Jeremy.

He stood in the doorway of the little room in the Enchanted Theater.

"Meow," said Aristotle from the top of a gold and blue trunk.

"At last!" said Mr. Magnus. He sat on a stool beside the window. He held a scroll made of thin parchment. "Come in! Come in!"

Jeremy's heart thumped. All the strange things that had happened yesterday were true! It wasn't just a dream!

He walked around the room. It looked almost the same. Bright costumes hung on racks. Silver swords and shields leaned against the walls. Zeus's lightning bolt gleamed in the corner. *Do Not Touch* signs dangled from strings.

But something was different.

Books!

Books rose in tall wobbly stacks everywhere. Books were piled on the windowsill. Books were scattered across the floor. Tattered markers stuck out from between the pages.

"Wow!" said Jeremy. "Where did all the books come from?"

"The library," said Mr. Magnus. "I signed out all the books on ancient Greek myths."

"To help you solve the riddle!" said Jeremy. He stared at the scroll. "So you can save the Enchanted Theater!"

The Enchanted Theater was in trouble. Every time Mr. Magnus tried to put on a play, lightning flashed. The power went out. All the people went home.

One night the lightning bolt was in the shape of

the letter Z. It was a sign from Zeus, the king of the ancient Greek gods.

Yesterday, Jeremy and Aristotle had traveled back in time three thousand years. They traveled to Mount Olympus to talk to Zeus.

Zeus said that Mr. Magnus was ruining the Greek myths. He mixed things up in the plays. He changed the endings.

Zeus gave Jeremy three scrolls. Each scroll had a riddle in it. Zeus said that when Mr. Magnus solved all three riddles, he would take away the curse on the Enchanted Theater.

"I've been reading the books all day," said Mr. Magnus, "but it hasn't helped."

"I'm good at riddles," said Jeremy. He stood beside Mr. Magnus. He read the words on the ancient scroll out loud: *"In the land of Hades by night and day, six blood-red lanterns light my way. Who am I?"*

Jeremy frowned. It was a hard riddle.

"Hades is the god of the Underworld," said Mr. Magnus helpfully. "He's in all the books." He sighed. "But the books don't say anything about blood-red lanterns."

"What's the Underworld?" said Jeremy.

"It's where all the dead people go," said Mr. Magnus.

"Oh," said Jeremy.

The Underworld sounded horrible. Jeremy shivered.

Aristotle twitched his tail back and forth. "Meow!" he said.

Mr. Magnus said, "I'm getting to that part, Aristotle."

"What part?" asked Jeremy. His neck prickled.

"It's Aristotle's idea," mumbled Mr. Magnus. "The two of you will go to the Underworld to find the blood-red lanterns."

"You mean travel back in time?" said Jeremy. "Again? To a place with dead people? No thanks!"

There was a long silence.

Jeremy sighed. "Okay, okay. But will you come with us this time?"

Mr. Magnus looked alarmed. "The Enchanted Theater Rule Book says—"

"I know," muttered Jeremy. "You have to be a hero to time travel."

He had felt like a hero yesterday. He had done five brave things to get back from Mount Olympus. But he didn't feel like a hero today. He just felt like Jeremy, a boy whose mother was expecting him home for supper.

The Rule Book also said that time travel happened at sunset. You held onto one of the actors' props and counted to ten.

Jeremy glanced out the little window. The sky was purple and pink.

For the first time, he noticed a long black whip leaning against a tower of books. "Is this the prop we're going to use?" he said.

"Wait! Don't touch!" screeched Mr. Magnus.

But it was too late. Jeremy had picked up the black whip. It was warm. His fingers tingled.

"You're not ready!" said Mr. Magnus. "I haven't shown you my map! I haven't told you about the ferryman and the three-headed dog—"

Everything swirled around Jeremy. Mr. Magnus slid something over his arms. It felt like a backpack. There was a thump on his shoulder. Soft fur brushed his cheek.

Aristotle whispered, "We're going!"

Then everything went black.

Chapter Two
Back in Time

Jeremy blinked. He was sitting beside a swamp. Green slime covered the murky water. Cold clammy fog tickled his face.

Jeremy had just traveled back in time three thousand years. He didn't look any different. He was still wearing his jeans and runners. He didn't feel any different. Except that he was stiff and cold.

He looked around for Aristotle. The cat was sitting on a mossy log, washing his fur.

"The Underworld sure is foggy," said Jeremy.

Aristotle stopped licking. "We aren't in the Underworld yet." He flicked his tail. "You better check the map."

"What map?" said Jeremy. Then he remembered the backpack that Mr. Magnus had slipped over his shoulders when they were leaving. He slid it off and unzipped it.

One by one, Jeremy took out all the things that Mr. Magnus had packed inside. He took out a bright red flashlight. He took out a peanut-butter-and-honey sandwich wrapped in wax paper. He took out a shiny silver flute.

Aristotle peered over his shoulder. Jeremy pulled out two gold coins. He slipped them into his pocket.

He dug to the bottom of the pack. He felt a stiff roll of paper.

Mr. Magnus's map!

Jeremy unrolled it. He spread it across his knees.

"This isn't a swamp," he said. "It's the River Styx. And we have to get to the other side!" He peered into the gloom. "Wherever that is!"

Splash splash splash.

Jeremy's heart jumped. He strained harder to see into the fog.

Splash splash splash.

Someone was coming across the river!

"Pretend to be dead!" hissed Aristotle.

"Whaaa?" said Jeremy.

"We want to get into the Underworld, don't we?"

Jeremy lay on his back. The ground felt cold and soggy. He closed his eyes. He tried not to breathe.

Bump.

Something hit the bank.

Squish squish squish.

Jeremy shuddered.

Who was coming?

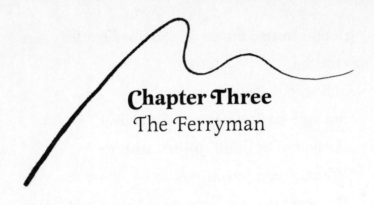

Chapter Three
The Ferryman

Jeremy took a big breath.

He opened his eyes. A man stared down at him. He had long straggly gray hair. His skin was white. He wore a dark oilskin coat and muddy boots.

Jeremy gulped. He tried to remember what Mr. Magnus had said. "You must be the ferryman," he stammered.

The man scowled. He looked like he was waiting for something.

Aristotle nudged Jeremy. The gold coins! Jeremy sat up and dug them out of his pocket. He gave them to the ferryman.

The ferryman's hands felt like damp leaves.

The coins disappeared into the folds of his long coat. Then he grunted, "Get in."

Jeremy looked around for the ferry. All he saw was an ancient rowboat. It was made of weathered gray boards. The boards looked rotten.

"Er...Does your boat ever leak?" said Jeremy.

The ferryman didn't say anything. He climbed into the boat. Jeremy crammed everything into the backpack. He scrambled into the boat. Aristotle hopped in after him.

The man hunched his shoulders and pushed against the pole. Pale green weeds trailed against the bow of the boat. A thin snake glided through the murky water. Two mud-brown eyes stared from a lily pad. Cold mist swirled around them. Jeremy hugged his arms. He was freezing.

He peered into the thick gray fog. After a long time the rowboat bumped against a bank. They had made it! Jeremy and Aristotle climbed out. The ferryman poled silently away.

"Wait!" called Jeremy. "Do you know where we can find six blood-red lanterns?"

But the ferryman had disappeared. Jeremy gazed around. The fog parted. A huge iron gate loomed out of the mist. In front of it was the biggest doghouse Jeremy had ever seen.

The three-headed dog.

The fur on Aristotle's back bristled.

"Don't worry," said Jeremy quickly. "I don't see anything moving. And it's awfully quiet. He's probably not home—"

A loud cracking sound made them both jump.

Aristotle shot between Jeremy's legs.

It was the sound of a giant dog crunching on giant bones.

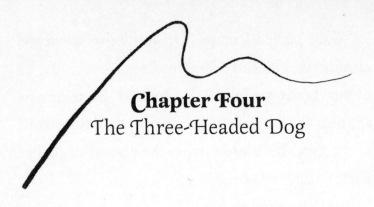

Chapter Four
The Three-Headed Dog

Jeremy and Aristotle hid in the middle of a bush.

CRACK! CRUNCH! SNAP!

"He guards the gate to the Underworld," whispered Aristotle. "He was in one of Mr. Magnus's books. He only lets you in if you're a shade."

"What's a shade?" said Jeremy.

"A dead person," said Aristotle.

"Great," said Jeremy. They had fooled the ferryman. But he didn't think they could fool the three-headed dog.

The gigantic doghouse rumbled and shook.

"He's coming out!" said Aristotle.

A huge, shaggy, black dog lumbered out of the dog house. The dog had three enormous heads. Its fiery red eyes glowed. Its white fangs glistened. Its huge hairy ears flapped like wings.

The monster turned its three heads from side to side.

Sniff! Sniff! Sniff!

Jeremy held his breath. The dog growled and lay down on its stomach.

Jeremy let his breath out.

"What else did it say in the book?" he whispered to Aristotle.

Aristotle sighed. "Only a few people who are alive have ever got past him into the Underworld. But I don't remember how they did it."

"Think!" said Jeremy.

Aristotle's tail twitched. "Mr. Magnus read a story about a man who wanted to visit his dead father. He gave the dog a honey cake. It put him to sleep."

Jeremy and Aristotle looked at each other.

The peanut-butter-and-honey sandwich!

Jeremy slid the backpack off his shoulders. He took out the peanut-butter-and-honey sandwich. He unwrapped it. The wax paper crackled.

"Shhhh," said Aristotle.

Jeremy glared at Aristotle.

Then he said, "Here goes!"

He crawled out of the bush. He inched forward on his hands and knees. He flung the sandwich in front of the dog. Then he scurried back to the bush.

The monster lifted its three heads.

Sniff! Sniff! Sniff!

Drool dripped from its three massive jaws. Then it flopped back down on the ground.

"He's not hungry," said Jeremy. "He ate too many bones."

"I know!" said Aristotle. "You could pretend to be Orpheus!"

"Who's Orpheus?" said Jeremy.

21

"A famous Greek musician. He was in Mr. Magnus's books too. Orpheus wanted to rescue his girlfriend from the Underworld. The three-headed dog stopped him at the gate. But Orpheus played such beautiful music that the dog fell asleep."

Jeremy and Aristotle looked at each other.

The silver flute!

Jeremy took out the flute. "Here I go again!" he said. He crawled out of the bush. His hands shook. He licked his lips. He blew into the flute.

WHOOSH! SQUEAK!

He blew harder. *SCREECH!*

The dog whined. Its huge ears drooped. Its red eyes blinked.

Jeremy looked back at Aristotle. "I don't know how to play a flute!" he hissed.

"Try singing," Aristotle hissed back.

Jeremy frowned. He couldn't remember any songs. Then he thought about the ferryman. He took a big breath. He sang in a loud voice:

"Row row row your boat
Gently down the stream
Merrily merrily merrily merrily
Life is but a dream."

Jeremy sang the song four more times. He peeked at the dog. Its eyes were shut. Deep grumbly snores rumbled from its three throats.

"It worked!" said Jeremy.

Aristotle bounded out beside him. "Come on!"

Jeremy and Aristotle ran past the sleeping monster. They ducked through the iron gate. They sped up a misty road between two steep hills.

"We'd better stop and look at the map," said Jeremy, panting.

Just then a shrill whinny rang through the mist.

There was a rattling noise.

And the sharp crack of a whip.

"Someone's coming!" said Aristotle. "Quick, Jeremy! Hide!"

Chapter Five
King of the Underworld

Jeremy and Aristotle jumped off the road. They scrambled up the hill and hid behind a boulder.

A black chariot pulled by two black horses burst through the mist. The horses had flowing black tails and manes. Red rubies sparkled on their harnesses.

A tall man drove the chariot. He wore a black helmet that glistened with diamonds. His black cape swirled in the wind. He cracked a long thin whip.

"That's Hades," said Aristotle. "He's the god of the Underworld."

Jeremy shivered.

"Whoa!" shouted Hades.

He pulled the reins. The horses reared. Smoke poured from their flared nostrils.

Hades stared up the side of the hill. He stared right at their boulder. His face was like cold stone.

Goose bumps prickled the back of Jeremy's neck. Then Hades looked the other way.

"He's searching for shades," whispered Aristotle. "Dead people. He wants to take them to his palace to be his slaves."

"Oh," said Jeremy. He tried to crunch into a tiny ball. His runner kicked against a loose rock. It rattled down the side of the hill.

Hades spun around. He looked right at Jeremy.

"Run!" shouted Aristotle.

Aristotle bounded up the steep hill. Jeremy scrambled after him. He grabbed onto tufts of grass to pull himself up.

Jeremy looked back.

The gray mist swirled around him. He could hear rocks sliding and heavy breathing.

Hades was coming after them!

And then, when Jeremy turned around, he couldn't see Aristotle!

He was in the middle of a thick gray cloud.

A voice squeaked, "Over here!"

The voice came from inside the hill. A large rock ledge jutted out in front of Jeremy. He crawled underneath into a tiny cave. Aristotle crouched at the back.

Jeremy squeezed beside Aristotle.

There was a loud crunching sound. A pair of huge black boots loomed right outside the cave.

Jeremy gulped.

They were close enough to touch!

Chapter Six
The Seven Sisters

Jeremy closed his eyes. He held his breath. When he opened his eyes, the boots were gone.

After a long time, Jeremy and Aristotle crept to the entrance of the cave. An eerie laugh floated up through the mist. A horse whinnied. Chariot wheels clattered away on the stony ground.

"Whew!" said Jeremy. "That was a close call."

Jeremy and Aristotle went back down the hill to the road. They walked for a long time. The land on either side of the road was flat and gray. An icy wind blew.

Jeremy checked the map. "This is called the Plains of Judgment." He shivered. "It's creepy here."

Just then he heard a soft rustling sound. He turned around. A man trudged up the road behind them.

"It's a shade," said Aristotle nervously. "Let him go by, and pretend you don't see him."

Jeremy frowned. The shade didn't look scary. He looked like a real person.

"Hello," called Jeremy boldly. "Can you tell me where I can find six blood-red lanterns?"

The man lifted his head. Jeremy gasped. The shade's face was twisted with pain. "I can't stop now," the shade whispered. He vanished past them into the mist.

Jeremy and Aristotle kept walking. More shades flitted past, their heads bent to the ground.

Suddenly Jeremy stopped. "Look!"

A little way from the road, seven women huddled around a big bronze tub beside a stream. Each woman held a bucket. Jeremy and Aristotle watched them fill the buckets in the stream and pour the water into the tub. The water ran out through seven large holes in the bottom of the tub. Wailing, the women filled their buckets from the stream again. Again, the water ran out of the tub!

"They're the daughters of a king," said Aristotle. "Mr. Magnus said we might meet them. They're being punished by Hades. They have to stay there until the tub is filled."

"That's awful!" said Jeremy. He took a big breath. "Excuse me!" he called.

"Don't do that!" cried Aristotle. "Hades won't like it if you—"

But Jeremy had run over to the women. "Why don't you plug the holes?" he suggested.

The seven sisters stared at him. Then one of the women nodded slowly. She tore a small strip from the bottom of her tunic. She stuffed the cloth into a hole. Her sisters did the same thing with the other holes.

"Now watch!" said Jeremy. He filled one of the

buckets from the stream. He poured the water into the tub. The water stayed in.

The seven sisters laughed and clapped their hands. "Dear boy, dear boy!" they cried. "We can fill the tub at last! We're free! How can we thank you?"

"Do you know where I can find six blood-red lanterns?" said Jeremy.

The women shook their heads. One of them said, "Queen Persephone will know."

"Yes, yes," chimed the others. "Queen Persephone will tell you."

Jeremy frowned. "Who's Queen Persephone?"

"The Queen of the Underworld," said a sister.

"Where can I find her?" said Jeremy.

But the women had hurried to the stream with their buckets.

"Thank you, anyway," called Jeremy. He waved goodbye. He and Aristotle kept walking.

"Next time," said Aristotle, "it would be much safer if you didn't—"

But Jeremy had stopped again. A small crowd of shades had gathered a short distance from the road. "What are they looking at?" said Jeremy.

"You can't help everybody!" said Aristotle quickly.

But Jeremy ran over to the shades. He stood on tiptoe and peered over their shoulders.

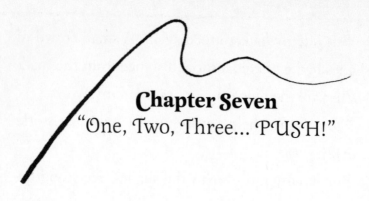

Chapter Seven
"One, Two, Three... PUSH!"

A man was pushing a huge boulder up the side of a steep hill. Sweat trickled down his back. His hands were bleeding.

He was almost at the top of the hill. The crowd was still. Then the boulder rolled backward, all the way back to the bottom of the hill. The crowd groaned. The man trudged wearily back down the hill. He started to push again.

"His name is Sisyphus," Aristotle whispered beside Jeremy. "He made Hades very angry. This is his punishment"

"That's terrible!" said Jeremy.

He took a big breath. "I'll help you!"

Jeremy ran forward. He stood beside Sisyphus and pushed the boulder. All the shades ran over too.

"One two three…PUSH!" shouted Jeremy.

Everybody pushed. The boulder inched up the hill.

"Harder!" gasped Jeremy.

The boulder rolled over the top of the hill. It disappeared down the other side.

The shades cheered. Sisyphus shook Jeremy's hand. "How can I thank you?"

"Can you tell me where I can find six blood-red lanterns?" said Jeremy.

Someone in the crowd shouted, "Ask Queen Persephone. Queen Persephone will know."

"But where is Queen Persephone?" said Jeremy.

Nobody heard him. The shades lifted Sisyphus on their shoulders. "Hip hip hooray!" they shouted.

Jeremy sighed. "Thank you, anyway."

Jeremy and Aristotle kept walking. After a long time, they came to a place where the road went two different ways.

Jeremy took the map out of his backpack. "We're right here," he said finally. He pointed to a place in the middle of the map.

Mr. Magnus had drawn two arrows at the fork in the road. He had written beside each arrow in his spidery printing. Jeremy looked at the first arrow. He read out loud, "To the Valley of Heroes."

The Valley of Heroes looked peaceful. Mr. Magnus had drawn pictures of flowers and birds and shades with big smiles.

Aristotle peered over his shoulder. "That's where all the dead heroes go," he said excitedly. "It was in one of Mr. Magnus's books." He purred. "They might even have feasts there. Let's go!"

Jeremy shook his head slowly. He wanted to go to the Valley of Heroes too. But they had to solve the riddle of the six blood-red lanterns.

Jeremy pointed to the second arrow on the map. He read out loud in a shaky voice, "To the Palace of Hades."

Chapter Eight
The Valley of Heroes

Jeremy looked at the map again. It was a long way to Hades' palace.

"We better rest here for a few minutes," he said. He looked up.

Aristotle was gone!

"Great!" said Jeremy. He jumped up. "Aristotle! Where did you go?"

Jeremy peered up the narrow dark road that led to the Palace of Hades. Then he looked along the road to the Valley of Heroes. Far away, a pale light glowed in the sky.

An orange tail disappeared around a bend.

"Aristotle!" yelled Jeremy.

He ran after Aristotle. Panting, he caught up to the cat at the fifth bend in the road. "What's the big idea? Where do you think you're going?"

Aristotle flicked his tail. "I just want to see the Valley of Heroes. Just one teeny tiny look. Just one—"

Jeremy sighed. The Valley of Heroes was probably just around the corner. "Oh, all right," he said.

He followed Aristotle. When they reached the last bend in the road, Jeremy stood still.

The Valley of Heroes was beautiful. The sun burst out of the gray gloom. Golden birds sang from the branches of trees. Unicorns with silver horns grazed beside a bubbling stream.

Men in white tunics were gathered around the edge of a large playing field. They were cheering and shouting.

"It's like Sports Day!" said Jeremy. "And those must be the heroes!"

Jeremy loved Sports Day. He raced to the edge of the crowd. He squeezed between the men.

Four runners sprinted down the track with sticks in their hands. The crowd roared. Someone pushed Jeremy forward.

Suddenly one of the racers passed him a stick. He was a huge man with big shoulders. "Run!" he shouted.

Jeremy ran. He ran like the wind. He ran all the way around the track. When he finally stopped, the crowd cheered.

"Hey, Hercules!" someone yelled. "Where did you get your friend?"

Hercules!

Jeremy looked around. The racer who had passed him the stick smiled at him. "Thanks, kid," he said. "You made us win."

"You're Hercules?" stammered Jeremy.

"That's right."

"Wow!" said Jeremy.

He had learned about Hercules at school. Hercules was a famous Greek hero!

"Come on!" said Hercules. "We're going to have a javelin throw next. You can be on my team again."

Jeremy shook his head sadly. Hercules was so cool. And he loved the Valley of Heroes. But they had to go to Hades' palace to find Queen Persephone.

Where was Aristotle?

He gazed around. He spotted Aristotle sitting in the grass beside a small clear blue pool.

Jeremy frowned. The pool looked familiar. He pulled out Mr. Magnus's map and stared at it. His heart thudded.

"The Pool of Forgetfulness," he read out loud.

Underneath, in his spidery printing, Mr. Magnus had written: *Where heroes drink to forget their past lives.*

"ARISTOTLE!" shouted Jeremy. "DON'T DRINK THE WATER!"

He ran to the pool.

"Whew!" he said. "Boy, was that ever close! Mr. Magnus said—"

Aristotle flicked his tail.

He rolled on his back and purred softly.

Then he said, "Do I know you?"

Chapter Nine
A Ride with Hercules

"It's me! Jeremy!" said Jeremy.

He groaned.

"Don't you remember? Mr. Magnus sent us here to find the six blood-red lanterns! So we can solve the riddle and save the Enchanted Theater!"

Aristotle looked at him politely. A crowd gathered around them, listening.

Jeremy's face went red. "Oh, never mind," he muttered. The important thing was to find Queen Persephone.

Just then the Valley of Heroes became deathly still. The golden birds stopped singing. The unicorns with silver horns bounded into a grove of trees.

The heroes fell silent. They stared at a black chariot and rider rattling at full speed along the road into the valley.

Hades, the god of the Underworld!

Hades stopped his horses in front of the Pool of Forgetfulness. He pulled his black cape tightly around his shoulders. A black visor shaded his eyes.

"He can't bear the sunlight," whispered a hero beside Jeremy.

The horses blew steam from their nostrils. They stamped their feet. Hades scanned the silent crowd. "I'm looking for a boy and an orange cat!" he roared.

A huge man with big shoulders stepped in front of Jeremy and Aristotle. It was Hercules! "We haven't seen them," he called back.

Jeremy held his breath. The heroes murmured in agreement. "Hercules is right. We haven't seen them," they shouted.

Hades glowered. He whipped the horses and spun the chariot around. He disappeared up the road in a thunder of galloping hooves.

"Thanks, Hercules," said Jeremy.

"I like to help a friend," said Hercules. He looked at the sun. "It's too late for the javelin throw. I have to go."

"Where are you going?" said Jeremy.

"To Mount Olympus," said Hercules. "That's where I live. The gods gave me everlasting life. I come here to the Underworld in my chariot once a month for the races."

"Oh," said Jeremy.

He thought fast.

"On your way out of the Underworld, do you go near the palace of Hades?"

Hercules looked at Jeremy closely. "I go right past."

Jeremy took a big breath.

He said, "Do you think you could give us a ride?"

Chapter Ten
The Palace of Hades

Hercules cracked his whip. His two white horses flew over the road. The wind blew in Jeremy's face.

As they left the Valley of Heroes, the sun disappeared. They were back in the cold and the mist. Jeremy shivered.

"We'll take the shortcut!" cried Hercules.

Huge wings unfolded on the sides of the horses. The chariot lifted into the gray sky.

"Don't look down!" said Aristotle.

But Jeremy looked. Far below, a road climbed like a snake through the dark forest. A black chariot sped over the road. It was so tiny it looked like a toy. They were beating Hades!

Hercules' chariot soared higher. They were heading to a huge black palace on top of a jagged mountain peak. The castle had two tall turrets and a massive wooden door.

Hercules circled over the palace. Then he landed on the rocky ground. "Hey, Jeremy, are you sure—?"

But Jeremy had climbed out of the chariot. Aristotle hopped down beside him.

"Good-bye!" said Jeremy. "Thank you!" He waved until Hercules and his snow white horses were a speck in the sky.

"I forget," said Aristotle. "Tell me again. Who are you? And what are we doing here?"

Jeremy groaned. Somehow he had to find a way to free Aristotle from the spell of forgetfulness. But there was no time now. They had to find Queen Persephone before Hades got back to the palace.

He sighed. "You just have to trust me. I'll explain everything later." He stared up at the palace. Then he pushed open the heavy door.

It was pitch black inside. Jeremy remembered that Mr. Magnus had put a flashlight in his backpack. He dug in the pack for the flashlight and turned it on. He blinked in the sudden brightness.

They were in a huge entrance hall with stone walls. Dark passageways ran in every direction.

It was like a maze. Jeremy swallowed. Where was Queen Persephone?

Jeremy and Aristotle wandered up and down the winding passageways.

After a long time, cool air brushed Jeremy's face. Slits of yellow light gleamed in the distance. He shone the flashlight in a circle. They were standing in a small courtyard open to the sky. The yellow lights were the glowing eyes of stone wolves that stood against the courtyard walls.

A tall tree grew in the middle of the courtyard. The branches were weighed down with dark red fruit. Jeremy's stomach rumbled. He walked over to the tree. He reached for a piece of the red fruit.

"I wouldn't do that," whispered someone in the darkness.

Jeremy froze.

"That's a pomegranate," said the voice. "It's the Forbidden Fruit of the Dead."

Chapter Eleven
Queen Persephone

A woman stepped out of the shadows. She wore a long black gown and a black crown with red jewels. Her face was pale and very beautiful.

"Queen Persephone!" said Jeremy. He bowed.

The queen smiled. She touched Jeremy's arm. Her hands felt like ice.

Jeremy swallowed. "I'm Jeremy," he stammered. "And this is Aristotle. Only he doesn't remember who he is."

"Ah," said Queen Persephone, "the Pool of Forgetfulness."

She laid her hands on Aristotle's head. She sang softly. The song was strange and haunting.

Aristotle's ears twitched. His tail stood straight up. He looked at Jeremy and blinked twice. "Isn't it time to go back to the Enchanted Theater?"

"Queen Persephone broke the spell!" said Jeremy.

He wanted to go home too. But they still hadn't found the six blood-red lanterns. And he wanted to learn more about this strange sad queen.

It was as if Queen Persephone had read his mind. "Sit with me, and I will tell you my story," she said.

She led Jeremy and Aristotle to a stone bench in the shadows. "I was captured by Hades when I was a young girl picking flowers. I was brought here against my will to be his queen."

"That's terrible!" said Jeremy.

Queen Persephone smiled sadly. "My mother is the goddess of the harvest. When she found out that Hades had stolen me, she punished the world by making it always winter. The earth was cold and barren for twelve months of the year."

"Zeus wouldn't like that!" said Aristotle.

"He didn't. He ordered Hades to send me home. But just when I was ready to leave the Underworld, I ate six seeds of a pomegranate."

"The Forbidden Fruit of the Dead!" said Jeremy.

"That's right," said Queen Persephone. "As a punishment, I must spend six months of every year as queen of the Underworld. That's when the earth has its winter. And when I go home to my mother for six months, the earth has summer."

Jeremy shuddered. He had almost eaten the Forbidden Fruit of the Dead too!

He looked at the queen's pale face. "But why do you sit here in the dark?" he said.

"The light bothers Hades," Queen Persephone said. She sighed. "He lets me have candles in my stone wolves. The candlelight shines through their eyes like lanterns."

She gazed longingly at Jeremy's flashlight. "I've never seen such a wonderful thing as that."

Jeremy stared at the glowing yellow eyes of the stone wolves. Queen Persephone was right.

The wolves' eyes looked just like lanterns!

Jeremy was sure it was a clue to the riddle. He said slowly, *"In the land of Hades by night and day, six blood-red lanterns light my way. Who am I?"*

He thought hard.

The six blood-red lanterns could be eyes! Six blood-red eyes! Why hadn't he thought of that before?

Jeremy's neck prickled. The dog that guarded the gate to Hades had three enormous heads. It had white fangs that glistened. It had huge hairy ears that flapped like wings. *It had six fiery red eyes.*

"I've solved the riddle!" he cried. "The answer is the three-headed dog!"

Aristotle jumped off the stone bench. He waved his tail. "Now we can go home," he purred.

"It says in the Enchanted Theater Rule Book that a hero must do five brave things to return home," said Jeremy slowly.

He counted on his fingers. "I pretended to the ferryman that I was dead. That's one."

He bit his lip. "I tricked the three-headed dog. That's two!" He thought hard. "I helped the king's daughters on the Plains of Judgment. That's three!"

"What else?" said Aristotle. He sounded worried.

"I helped Sisyphus push the boulder over the hill!" said Jeremy. "That's four!"

THUD! THUD! THUD!

Heavy footsteps echoed in the passageway that led to the courtyard. Jeremy and Aristotle stared at each other.

"PERSEPHONE!" bellowed a gruff voice.

"Hades is coming!" said Queen Persephone. "Quick! I'll show you another way out."

She led Jeremy and Aristotle to a second passageway on the far side of the courtyard.

"Good luck," she whispered.

Chapter Twelve
Home Again

Jeremy turned off his flashlight. He and Aristotle slipped into the darkness. "Have you thought of the fifth brave thing yet?" said Aristotle.

Jeremy didn't answer. His head spun. Queen Persephone was kind. She had broken the spell of forgetfulness. She had stopped Jeremy from eating the Forbidden Fruit of the Dead. She had given them the clue to the riddle.

He hated to think of her sitting in that gloomy courtyard. He looked at his flashlight. He made up his mind. He and Aristotle would have to find their way out of the palace in the dark.

He stepped back into the courtyard.

THUD! THUD! THUD!

Hades was almost there! Jeremy took a big breath. He ran across the courtyard. He slipped the flashlight into Queen Persephone's icy hand. "You can keep it," he said quickly. "You need it more than I do."

Queen Persephone's face lit up with joy.

"Don't leave it on when you're not using it," warned Jeremy. "Or else the batteries—"

Just then, everything swirled around him. He closed his eyes. Aristotle landed with a thump on his shoulder.

A voice roared, "The boy and the orange cat? What are they doing here?"

Aristotle squeaked in fright.

And then everything went black.

Jeremy opened his eyes. He was standing in the middle of the little room in the Enchanted Theater. Aristotle sat on top of the blue and gold trunk.

Mr. Magnus peered at Jeremy.

"I know what the fifth brave thing was," said Jeremy. "I went back to the courtyard to give Queen Persephone the flashlight."

Mr. Magnus blinked. "Yes, yes," he said. "But did you solve the riddle?"

He waved the scroll at Jeremy.

"The answer is the three-headed dog!" said Jeremy. "His six red eyes are like lanterns. Queen Persephone's stone wolves gave me the idea. And then I thought—"

But Mr. Magnus wasn't listening. He stared at the lightning bolt in the corner of the room. It glowed with sudden dazzling light.

"Zeus's lightning bolt!" said Jeremy. "What does it mean?"

"I think it means it's the right answer!" said Mr. Magnus.

Jeremy sighed. "Do you think Hades will let Queen Persephone keep the flashlight?"

"I think so," said Mr. Magnus. "In all the books it says that Hades loves his queen and treats her well."

"I'm glad," said Jeremy. He looked at the little window. The sky was purple and pink. Time had stood still while he and Aristotle were time-traveling. He wasn't too late for supper. And he was still hungry!

"I better go home," he said.

"Will you come back tomorrow?" said Mr. Magnus, "to help solve the second riddle?"

"Sure," said Jeremy. "I'm great at riddles."

He went to the door of the little room. "So long, Mr. Magnus! See you later, Aristotle!"

"Good-bye!" said Mr. Magnus.

"Meow," said Aristotle.

He twitched his tail and purred.

Becky Citra is the author of *Jeremy and the Enchanted Theater*, the first book in the Jeremy series. She is also author of the Max and Ellie books, Orca Young Readers set in nineteenth-century Upper Canada. She lives in Bridge Lake, British Columbia.

Jeremy and Aristotle's
adventures continue in
Jeremy and the Golden Fleece.

Jeremy has more riddles to solve.

Where will he and Aristotle travel next?